MATCH WITS WITH

SHERLOCK HOLMES

Volume 3

MATCH WITS
WITH
SHERLOCK HOLMES

The Adventure of the Six Napoleons

The Blue Carbuncle

adapted by
MURRAY SHAW
from the original stories by Sir Arthur Conan Doyle

illustrated by GEORGE OVERLIE

Carolrhoda Books, Inc./Minneapolis

To young mystery lovers everywhere

The author gratefully acknowledges permission granted by Dame Jean Conan Doyle to use the Sherlock Holmes characters and stories created by Sir Arthur Conan Doyle.

Library of Congress Cataloging-in-Publication Data

Shaw, Murray.
Match wits with Sherlock Holmes. The Adventure of the Six Napoleons. The Blue Carbuncle / adapted by Murray Shaw from the original stories by Sir Arthur Conan Doyle : illustrated by George Overlie.
p. cm. — (Match wits with Sherlock Holmes : v. 3)
Summary: Presents two adventures of Sherlock Holmes and Dr. Watson, each accompanied by a section identifying the clues mentioned in the story and explaining the reasoning used by Holmes to put the clues together and come up with a solution. Also includes a map highlighting the sites of the mysteries.
ISBN 0-87614-387-7
1. Children's stories. English. [1. Mystery and detective stories. 2. Literary recreations.] I. Doyle. Arthur Conan. Sir, 1859-1920. II. Overlie, George, ill. III. Title. IV. Series: Shaw, Murray, Match wits with Sherlock Holmes : v. 3.
PZ7.S53426Si 1990
[Fic]—dc20 89-22293
CIP
AC

Manufactured in the United States of America

2 3 4 5 6 7 8 9 10 99 98 97 96 95 94 93 92 91

CONTENTS

In the year 1887, Sir Arthur Conan Doyle created two characters who captured the imagination of mystery lovers around the world. They were Sherlock Holmes—the world's greatest fictional detective—and his devoted companion, Dr. John H. Watson. These characters have never grown old. For over a hundred years, they have delighted readers of all ages.

In the Sherlock Holmes stories, the time is always the late 1800s and the setting, Victorian England. Holmes and Watson live in London, on the second floor of 221 Baker Street. When Holmes travels through back alleys and down gaslit streets to solve crimes, Watson is often at his side. After Holmes's cases are complete, Watson records them. These are the stories of their adventures.

INTRODUCTION

Sherlock Holmes often learned about people by looking carefully at their belongings. One evening when Holmes and Watson were out, a visitor called and absentmindedly left his walking stick. When the two returned, they examined this evidence. Watson recalls:

The stick was made of oak, with a carved head. Just below the sculpted knob lay a wide silver band, and upon it was engraved: "To James Mortimer, M.D. from his friends of the C. C. H. 1884."

"Since we have missed this man Mortimer," Holmes

said to me, "maybe you can detect something about him from his walking stick."

Eager to take the challenge, I began, "The stick is worn down on the end, and therefore, I suggest this man is probably a village doctor who visits his patients on foot. I'd also propose that Dr. Mortimer is a middle-aged or elderly gentleman who was given this stick by the local hunting club. The *H* would then stand for hunt."

"Really, my dear Watson," said Holmes cheerfully, "you've outdone yourself. Now let me take a look." Pulling out his magnifying glass, he inspected the cane.

"I'd agree that he is a village doctor, but it's more likely that a hospital would present a doctor with an award than a hunting club. So I assume that *C. C. H.* stands for Charing Cross Hospital. And since older men seldom go from hospitals to country practices, Dr. Mortimer was probably a young doctor when he was given this stick. He would probably be in his mid-thirties at present."

"That seems reasonable," I admitted.

"And I'd also suggest that he has a dog because of the teeth marks on the stick," Holmes added. "The marks are too closely spaced for a mastiff and too far apart for a terrier. Thus, I suspect Dr. Mortimer has a spaniel." Hearing a noise, Holmes glanced out the window. "Actually, Watson," he continued with triumph, "I would say a curly-haired spaniel. Just look at the dog on our stoop."

Following his eyes, I saw the dog and the man he had just described. I laughed. Holmes's accurate eye and keen reasoning had once again revealed the truth.

"A dark figure, quick as a monkey, dashed up the path and disappeared into the deep shadow of the house."

THE ADVENTURE OF THE SIX NAPOLEONS

From time to time, Inspector Lestrade of Scotland Yard would drop by Baker Street for a quiet chat. Holmes welcomed these visits because they allowed him to keep up with the news at police headquarters.

On this particular June evening, Lestrade sat puffing silently on his cigar, looking troubled.

"Care to talk about it, Inspector?" asked Holmes. "You seem puzzled."

"As a matter of fact, I am, Mr. Holmes," said the inspector. "But the case I have in mind seems to have more to do with madness than with crime. Why would anyone sane go around smashing images of Napoleon?"

Holmes straightened up, sensing the opening of an interesting case. "I suggest that you start at the beginning of this, Inspector."

"My apologies," the inspector said, laughing at himself, "I often tell a story back end first." Setting his cigar down, he pulled out his notebook. "The first incident in this case occurred four days ago at Mr. Morse Hudson's art shop on Kennington Road. A clerk was in the back room when he heard a loud crash. He rushed into the front of the shop to find the place empty and a plaster cast of Napoleon's head lying in pieces on the floor.

"The bust had stood on a shelf with several other statues, but the others had not been harmed. Mr. Hudson decided that a customer must have knocked the statue over accidentally and fled. Since the incident seemed too trivial to report, Mr. Hudson just mentioned it to the local constable.

"The second occurrence," Lestrade continued, "happened last night. A well-known surgeon, Dr. Barnicot, lives not far from Mr. Hudson's shop. The doctor is a great admirer of Napoleon, and a few months ago he purchased two identical busts of Napoleon from Mr. Hudson. The doctor placed one in his home and the other in his clinic on Lower Brixton Road.

"This morning Dr. Barnicot awoke and came downstairs only to discover his first bust was missing. He searched the house and found that a burglar had carried the bust outside and smashed it against the garden wall. Nothing else was missing or destroyed."

"This is interesting indeed," said Holmes.

"Ah, but there's more," Lestrade added. "When Dr. Barnicot went into his office, he found the second bust in pieces, smashed right where it stood."

"Were these two busts the same type as the one smashed in Mr. Hudson's shop?"

"Yes, exactly. Mr. Hudson said that all three were from the same mold. He purchased them together over a year ago," said the inspector. "I can only assume this is the work of someone with a deep hatred of Napoleon . . . or a madman."

"I beg to differ with you, Inspector," said Holmes.

"There seems to be a method to this madness. So far this criminal has attacked only one type of image of Napoleon—a plaster bust. No, there is more to this."

"What are your conclusions then, Mr. Holmes?"

"I have none as yet," he answered thoughtfully. "But there's a pattern here. And I'm quite sure we haven't heard the last of this case."

It wasn't long before Holmes's prediction came true. The next morning our landlady entered with a telegram for Holmes.

"Watson, it's from Lestrade," said Holmes. "Would you be so kind as to order a cab? Then we'll find out why the inspector has taken to sending urgent telegrams."

Within a quarter of an hour, our cab pulled up at Pitt Street, a lane of plain row houses, dingy with dirt and soot. The police and a group of onlookers were standing around the middle house, number 131.

Holmes whistled under his breath. "By Jove, Watson, this must be a murder at the very least. Nothing less could hold such a crowd."

Lestrade caught sight of us and came down the walk. "I'm certainly glad you both could come," the inspector said. "The case of the busts has turned into a case of murder."

Lestrade led us up the steps to the front door. The landing was wet, and it was obvious that the police had just finished washing it down. Inside number 131, an elderly man in his flannel dressing gown was pacing.

"Are you reporters?" he asked suspiciously.

"No," said the inspector, "this is Mr. Sherlock Holmes and his friend Dr. John Watson. They are aiding us in the investigation."

The man strode back and forth in front of us, clearly upset. "I'm Horace Harker from the Central Press Syndicate," he said dramatically. "All my life I've been trying to be the first reporter with a story. Now a murder happens on my very own doorstep, and I can't even get the facts straight."

"What do you remember?" inquired Holmes.

"Last night near 3 a.m.," the reporter answered, "I heard an agonized scream from downstairs. It was the most horrible sound I have ever heard. For a while I waited, frozen with fear, and then I pulled a poker

from the fireplace and started creeping downstairs. The parlor window was open, and this cheap bust of Napoleon I had was missing. I ran out the front door but stumbled over something lying on the steps. Lighting a candle, I found a man with his throat cut. Oh . . . that poor man will haunt my dreams!" A sweat broke out on his forehead. "I started to blow my police whistle," he continued, "but I must have fainted. When I awoke, the police were here. They had taken the body to the morgue."

"Do you know who the man was?"

"I have no idea," said Harker, shaking his head.

Lestrade filled in the details for us. "The victim was a fairly tall man, dark haired and thick chested. A small, bloody knife was found lying next to him. There is no way, though, of telling if it was in fact the murder weapon. In the man's pockets, we found a London map, a half-eaten apple, a few coins, and this photograph."

Lestrade handed Holmes a crumpled picture of a man with thick black eyebrows and large features. His square mouth and chin jutted forward, and he was missing some front teeth.

"Do you recognize this man?" Holmes asked.

"No, I'm afraid I don't," Mr. Harker replied.

"And what happened to the bust?"

"We found it in front of an empty house down the street," said Lestrade. "Like the others, the bust was smashed to pieces. And once again it was the same kind of bust as the others. Mr. Harker had purchased it at the Harding Brothers' shop here in Kensington."

"I would like to examine the pieces, if I may, Inspector," said Holmes.

"Certainly," said Lestrade. "This way, please."

A few doors away, plaster pieces were scattered all around upon the grass. Holmes examined each piece.

"Inspector," he said solemnly, "when a man's life is worth less than one of these plaster busts, there's more at stake than meets the eye. It's interesting that the burglar did not break the bust inside Harker's house or near any of the houses closer to Harker's. Instead, he carried it to here under the lamp post, where he could see what he was doing."

Lestrade and I looked at each other, embarassed. We had not even noticed the lamp post.

"By George, Mr. Holmes," said the inspector, "that's it. All of the busts were broken in places where there was light. But what do you make of that fact?"

"Nothing certain yet. But we need to take note of it for the future."

"Unfortunately, Mr. Holmes," said the inspector reluctantly, "I cannot waste any more of my time on these busts. I must identify the dead man so I can figure out why he was murdered."

"Quite so, Inspector," said Holmes, "but I think I'll follow a different line of investigation. If it is convenient, kindly meet us at Baker Street at 6 p.m. and we'll compare our findings."

"An excellent idea," Lestrade replied, walking back.

"Inspector," Holmes called out after him, "could you

tell Mr. Harker that I think the murderer is a madman with a hatred of Napleon?"

"You don't believe that, do you?" I asked, confused.

Holmes smiled. "Don't I? Perhaps, perhaps not. At any rate it would be useful for his article," said Holmes, looking smug.

The inspector just shrugged. "I'll pass on the message."

After the inspector left, Holmes began walking up to High Street. "If you ask me, Holmes," I said, keeping pace with him, "I think we need more facts."

"There's no doubt about that, my dear Watson," said Holmes. "We must trace the busts to their source. That's why we're heading for the shop where Mr. Harker bought his Napoleon."

Unfortunately, when we reached Harding Brothers, the clerk told us that he was new and had no information for us. He advised us to return in the afternoon when one of the brothers would be in.

"I suppose we can't expect everything to come easily," murmured Holmes, frustrated. "We'd best make our way to Hudson's shop on Kennington Road."

Once there, our luck improved. Morse Hudson was in and ready to talk. "What we pay taxes for I just don't know," he complained in a peppery manner. "Ruffians can come in and smash people's property and never be heard from again. It's a disgrace!"

"Exactly," said Holmes. "Now, could you tell me where you purchased the bust that was smashed in your shop and the two you sold to Dr. Barnicot?"

Hudson groaned and pulled at his gray mustache. "Well, what good will that do you? You should be out looking for the scoundrel—not going backwards and bothering a perfectly respectable house of trade. It was Gelder and Company on Church Street. I've been doing business with them for twenty years."

Holmes smiled, happy to have some data. He showed Hudson the photograph taken from the dead man's pocket and asked if the man in it looked familiar.

"Why, that's Beppo!" Hudson exclaimed. "He worked here as my clerk for the last few weeks, and an unreliable chap he was. But an excellent craftsman. You couldn't find better. Even so, I haven't seen him in the last couple of days, and he'll find no work with me when he returns. I've washed my hands of him."

Holmes thanked Hudson, and we left. We hailed a cab for south London and traveled along the river Thames to the dock district. Here we found Gelder and Company. Enormous statues filled the yard outside the warehouse. Inside the building, fifty or so workmen were carving stone or molding plaster. As we entered, a large, blond man introduced himself as the manager. When we asked about the busts of Napoleon, he replied, "We make hundreds of that particular Napoleon bust each year. Here, I'll show you how it's done."

He walked us around the shop, pointing out how each bust is cast in two side sections. Later these two sides are joined with plaster along the nose and set in the hall to dry.

After this tour the manager checked his books. "The

three busts that went to Morse Hudson's shop were cast in a batch of six," he said. "They were finished in May and sent to him in June. The remaining three in the batch were sent to Harding Brothers."

"And would you know this man?" Holmes asked, showing the manager Beppo's photograph.

"Ah, that rascal!" shouted the man, his face growing red. "He has caused me plenty of trouble. He was one of my best workmen. But then one day he stabbed someone in the street and came running in here to hide. The police were right behind him and caught him a few minutes later. Of course he went to prison for the stabbing, but he only got a year. He's probably out by now."

As Holmes listened, a half smile played around the corner of his mouth. "And on what date did this stabbing take place?"

"I'm not sure, but his last check was on May 20."

"I see. Can you tell us anything more about this fellow?" Holmes inquired.

"No, but a cousin of his works for us. I dare say he could tell you more about him."

"No, no," cried Holmes, "not a word to the cousin, I beg you. It is absolutely essential to keep this quiet. Thank you for all your trouble."

As we walked out of the warehouse, Holmes was taking long strides. "We're on the right track now, Watson," he said. "We just need to keep following it. Let's head back to Harding Brothers now and find out where those last two busts are located."

"But, Holmes," I said, "what have a murder and stabbing to do with these busts? Do you suppose that Beppo is some kind of spy? Maybe something came in from the docks and was hidden in one of the busts."

Holmes smiled. "Nothing is ruled out yet, Watson. The sooner we locate the remaining busts, the sooner we'll have the information we need."

On the way to Harding Brothers, we took in a quick lunch at a small pub. Our attention was attracted by the headlines at a newsstand: *"KENSINGTON SLASHING. MADMAN MURDERS OUT OF HATE FOR NAPOLEON."*

Holmes and I chuckled. Horace Harker had finally written the big story he wanted, and it was sweeping London. Once the murderer read it, he would never suspect that Holmes was hot on his trail.

We arrived at Harding Brothers near closing time, and fortunately, one of the brothers was in. He checked his books and informed us that the shop had sold the other two busts—one to Mr. Josiah Brown of Chiswick and the other to a Mr. Jacob Sandeford of Reading.

"Are you and your brother the only ones who see these books?" asked Holmes.

Harding looked puzzled. "Why, yes. But it's strange that you should ask. A few days ago, I came back from lunch and found them scattered on the floor. Since then we've kept them under lock and key."

"A good practice," remarked Holmes.

We left the store and hurried back to Baker Street. The inspector was already there, pacing up and down impatiently. He looked like a rooster about to crow.

"Had any luck, Mr. Holmes?" he asked smugly.

"We've discovered the whereabouts of the remaining busts," Holmes responded coolly.

"Busts, busts! All you're worried about are those busts!" cried Lestrade, strutting around the room. "I've done better than that! I've identified the murdered man and found the reason for his death."

"Pray, Inspector, tell all," Holmes said, enjoying Lestrade's boasts.

"The dead man was Pietro Venucci, a known cut-throat from Naples. Scotland Yard had been watching him for a while. Last year about this time, he had been stabbed in a street fight, but he must have recovered. Evidently, someone sent Venucci to kill the man in the photograph. The man must have suspected that he was being followed and ambushed Venucci. Now, what do you think of that, Mr. Holmes?"

Holmes clapped his hands. "Excellent, Inspector. But I still have one question. What about the busts?"

"A minor point, Mr. Holmes," Lestrade answered. "It's merely a bizarre case of theft. Tonight I am going to begin tracking the murderer. Would either of you like to accompany me?"

"I would, Inspector, but I fancy there's a quicker way to catch him. Meet us at the home of Mr. Josiah Brown of Chiswick this evening, and you'll have a one-in-two chance of catching the man you seek."

Lestrade shook his head in good humor. "This sounds unlikely, but I've put up with your whims before, Mr. Holmes, and I may as well see where this one leads."

"At eleven then," Holmes said, "and I caution you to remain hidden until we arrive."

After Lestrade left, Holmes sent a letter by express messenger to Mr. Brown of Chiswick informing him of our evening plans. Then he sent a telegram to Mr. Sandeford of Reading, asking him to come to Baker Street the next day.

"Watson, since Chiswick is nearer than Reading, you can bet Beppo will show up in Chiswick first."

"But why does he want the busts?" I asked.

"That is the crucial question. And that's what I'm going to find out." Going to the storeroom, he pulled out a pile of old newspapers. "Watson," he said, "would you be so kind as to help me sort through these newspapers? We are looking for the ones from late April and May of last year. They should give us the information we need."

Once we had sorted them into piles, Holmes went to work alone, looking through each paper for something only he could know. As it neared ten-thirty, I began to wonder if he was looking in vain. But suddenly, he jumped up. "Watson, I've got it!" he cried. "And now we must be off, for Beppo's an impatient man—and dangerous. You'd best bring your revolver."

So in due haste, Holmes and I headed for the street and hailed a cab. About a block from Brown's house, Holmes had the cabby stop the carriage, and we walked the rest of the way. The darkness and fog of the night were settling in, and as we neared Brown's home, Lestrade appeared from behind a hedge.

Silently, the three of us crept to the back of the house. A small circle of light shone above the door.

"I fear we may have a long wait," whispered Holmes as we crouched low behind the garden hedge.

Fortunately, that didn't turn out to be the case. Not long after he said this, we heard the garden gate swing open. A dark figure, quick as a monkey, dashed up the path and disappeared into the deep shadow of the house. For a few moments all was quiet and then a gentle creaking sound told us a window was being opened. Silence followed. A few minutes later, a light flashed in one window and went out, and then appeared in another. The intruder was searching the house.

Just as we considered following him, the shadowy figure emerged from the back door. He was carrying a large white object. He set it down and and struck it hard with a club. A muffled crack, followed by a clatter of fragments, announced that this bust had been broken like the first four.

Absorbed in examining the pieces, the thief did not hear our approach. Holmes pounced like a tiger, tackling him from behind. As Lestrade clapped handcuffs on him, the man roared in anger and tried to bite Lestrade's hand. I pulled out my revolver and put it to the small of his back. He soon settled down. His face was twisted, but it was clearly Beppo, the man in the photograph.

With Beppo captured, Holmes went straight to the fragments on the path. He held each piece carefully up to the light. His shoulders sank in disappointment.

"Nothing here," he said. "Mr. Sandeford must have the bust we want."

Beppo glared, and Lestrade pushed the criminal toward the street. A whistle brought the cabby.

"Mr. Holmes," said the inspector, "it's too late now for explanations, but I want the full story soon."

Holmes smiled. "Come to our lodgings at 6 p.m. tomorrow, and all will be made clear."

At six o'clock the next evening, Lestrade was sitting in our parlor, waiting for an explanation. Just then a knock came at our door, and Holmes rose to answer it. In walked an elderly gentleman with a bulky package under his arm.

"I believe you are Mr. Holmes," he said. "Am I correct in thinking that you have offered to pay ten pounds for a bust of Napoleon?"

"You are," said Holmes.

"Well, Mr. Holmes, I am an honest man, and that is a princely sum compared to what I paid for it."

"Nevertheless," said Holmes graciously, "my offer still stands. I believe that is the bust you have there? Excellent! Now if you'll be good enough to sign this receipt, we may conclude our business."

Smiling broadly, Sandeford signed the receipt. Then he pocketed the ten pounds and left before Holmes could change his mind.

As soon as he had disappeared, Holmes spread a clean sheet over the table. Onto it he placed the last of the six busts and gave it a sharp tap with his riding crop. The bust shattered into fragments. Eagerly he inspected each piece. Then, with a cry of triumph, he held up a small splinter of plaster.

In the lamplight we could see a small, round, dark object sitting in the plaster like a plum in pudding.

"Gentleman," Holmes said formally, "let me introduce you to the fabulous black pearl of the Borgias. One man has already died for it, and who knows how many more will risk their lives to gain it."

Lestrade was staring at Holmes, his mouth open in astonishment. "How did it get there?"

Holmes was at his finest. "It was stolen from the Prince of Colonna when he was in London about a year ago. I found the account in the newspapers last night. At that time Scotland Yard suspected the princess's maid, who had a brother in London. But no firm evidence was found. The woman's name was Lucia Venucci."

I gasped. "Pietro's sister! Then Venucci helped his sister with the theft."

"Precisely, Watson," said Holmes. "I suspect that Beppo was once a friend of the two Venuccis. But greed overcame him. Beppo stabbed Pietro and stole the pearl. He knew he was being followed, so he ran

to Gelder and Company and into the drying hall. He pushed the pearl into one of the busts and covered it up before the police caught him. Once Beppo was out of prison, he went to work looking for the busts. From his cousin, Beppo was able to find out who had purchased the busts from Gelder and Company. Beppo then got a job at Mr. Hudson's. As a clerk, he could easily break the bust in the store without anyone seeing him. He could also find out who had purchased Mr. Hudson's other two Napoleons. Once he had taken care of the three busts from Mr. Hudson's shop, he headed for Harding Brothers. There he stole a look at the books while everyone was gone for lunch."

Holmes paused. "By this time Venucci was looking for Beppo, and Beppo must have realized it. So he killed Venucci at Mr. Harker's and then went back to his search for the remaining busts. Only two then remained: Mr. Brown's and Mr. Sandeford's. And you know the story from there."

"Remarkable, Mr. Holmes," said Lestrade in awe. "You have managed to solve three cases at once—the broken busts, the stolen pearl, and the murder. You are truly amazing."

Holmes seemed both proud of his accomplishment and embarassed by the attention.

"Lestrade," he said formally, "here is the Borgia Pearl. If you should come across another perplexing case, I would be happy to be of assistance."

Holmes figured out that a pearl in the hand is worth six smashed busts. Were you able to follow his reasoning? Check the **CLUES** *to see if you put the facts together as he did. With this case behind you, you'll be ready for the challenges of the next adventure.*

CLUES

that led to the solution of *The Adventure of the Six Napoleons*

Lestrade believed that the bust smasher hated Napoleon. Holmes, however, suspected that it was the bust itself that was important, not Napoleon. The thief seemed to be looking for a particular bust out of a group of look-alikes. This theory was confirmed when Holmes discovered that all the broken busts had been cast from the same mold in a batch of six.

Holmes noticed that all the busts were broken where there was enough light to examine the pieces. This made him think that the criminal was looking for something of value hidden in one of the busts—such as a jewel, coin, or document.

Holmes used Beppo's photo to get information. When Hudson recognized Beppo as his clerk, Holmes knew that the murder was definitely connected to the busts. Since Beppo had been a clerk in the shop at the time of the bust smashing, he was a suspect for both the murder and the thefts.

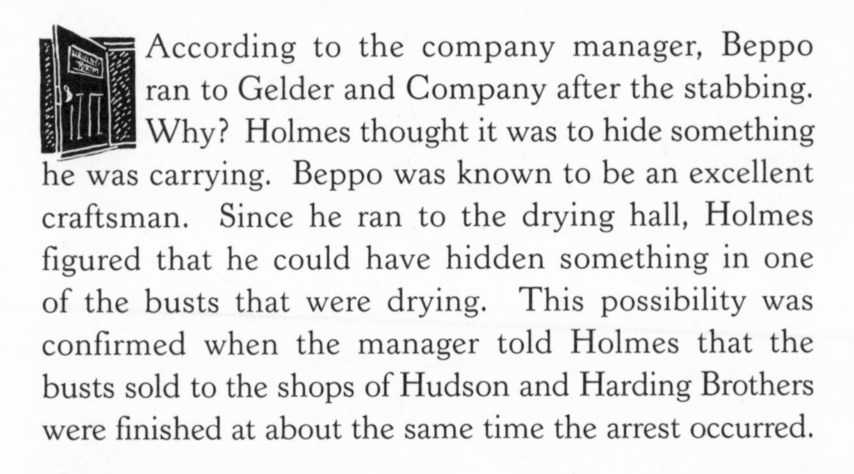

According to the company manager, Beppo ran to Gelder and Company after the stabbing. Why? Holmes thought it was to hide something he was carrying. Beppo was known to be an excellent craftsman. Since he ran to the drying hall, Holmes figured that he could have hidden something in one of the busts that were drying. This possibility was confirmed when the manager told Holmes that the busts sold to the shops of Hudson and Harding Brothers were finished at about the same time the arrest occurred.

The question remained: What was hidden in one of the busts? Holmes searched the newspapers of the previous spring to find a crime that had occurred near the time that Beppo had been arrested. The theft of the Borgia Pearl was exactly what he was looking for. Holmes's hunch was confirmed when he read that the maid's name was Lucia Venucci and that she had a brother in London. Holmes knew at once that Pietro Venucci must be the maid's brother.

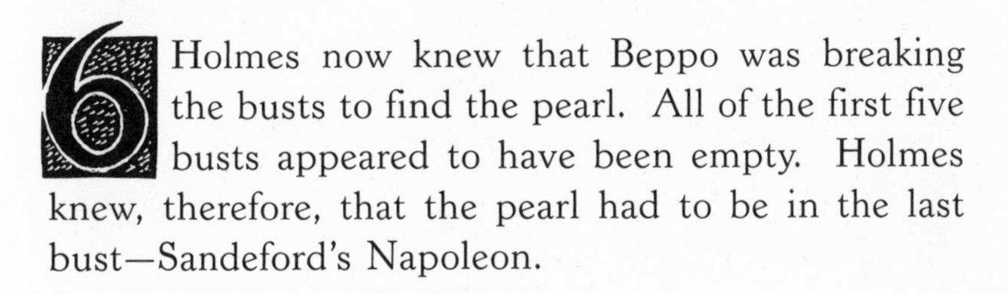

Holmes now knew that Beppo was breaking the busts to find the pearl. All of the first five busts appeared to have been empty. Holmes knew, therefore, that the pearl had to be in the last bust—Sandeford's Napoleon.

"The old man swung his stick at the ruffians but missed, shattering a store window instead."

THE BLUE CARBUNCLE

The morning after Christmas, 1889, was bitterly cold, and after visiting one of my patients, I was happy to come into the warmth of the lodgings on Baker Street. When I entered, I found Holmes sitting near the fire in his purple dressing gown. He was studying an old black hat with a magnifying glass and a pair of forceps.

"Ah, Watson," he called out cheerfully, "come have a look at this, and tell me what you make of it."

"I suspect that this has a gruesome story attached to it," I remarked.

Sherlock Holmes began to laugh. "No, my good doctor, this is something far more commonplace. You remember Peterson, the train attendant? He brought this trophy to me this morning, along with a plump Christmas goose. He told me that he had been on his way home from a holiday gathering at about three o'clock on Christmas morning. At Tottenham Court Road and Goodge Street, he saw a tall, elderly man stagger around the corner. The man had a goose slung over his shoulder, and some hoodlums tried to take the goose from him. In the scuffle one of them knocked his hat off. The old man swung his stick at the ruffians but missed, shattering a store window instead. Peterson ran to help the old man, and at the sight of his uniform, the young thugs went running, but so did the old man. The gentleman even dropped his goose."

"So Peterson got the prizes?" I asked.

"Yes, but being the honest fellow he is, he wanted to return them. So he brought them to me. The goose had a black tail feather and a card tied to its leg. The card said, *'For Mrs. Henry Baker.'* Peterson thought that with these clues I would be able to find the owner. But since there are hundreds of Henry Bakers in the city, it will not be an easy task."

"And what became of the goose?"

Holmes smiled. "It had to be eaten, so I sent it home with Peterson to be roasted."

I looked at the hat hanging on the back of the chair. It looked tattered and seedy. "What can anyone tell from examining a battered old hat?" I asked doubtfully.

Holmes sat back, watching me. "Quite a bit, my dear Watson," he said, "if you know what to look for. What can you gather from it?"

I took the hard felt hat into my hands. It was plain and round, with the brims turned up. Inside, the initials *H. B.* were scrawled on the red silk lining, which had darkened with age. The topside of the bowler was cracked, dusty, and spotted in several places. Yet there had been some effort to hide the spots by smearing them with ink.

"I see nothing unusual or important, Holmes," I said, handing it back to him. "It's just a hat."

Holmes shook his head. "On the contrary, Watson. You see everything, but you are not bold enough to put the facts together."

Holmes propped the hat on the end of his raised

finger. "First, judging by the size of the hat, the owner must be a smart man." Flippantly, Holmes set the hat on his head. It slipped down his forehead to cover his eyes and rest on the bridge of his nose.

"You see," said Holmes, "anyone with a head this large must have something in it."

I laughed at his ridiculous antics. "And what else can you deduce?"

"About three years ago, this man was quite well off, but he has fallen onto hard times since then."

"What makes you say that?"

"This style of hat with a curled brim was in fashion three years ago. And it was very expensive. Only a rich man could have afforded to buy such a hat. Yet," Holmes continued, "this hat is worn out. So the owner must not have the money to replace it at present. And though this man has fallen on hard times, he still has kept some self-respect."

"Why do you say that?" I asked.

"The stains on the hat have been covered with ink. This proves that he makes an effort to keep up his appearance." Holmes paused and then tossed the hat to me. "And surely you would agree, Watson, that this man does not go out often. And also that his wife no longer cares about him?"

"Certainly, you are joking, Holmes," I said.

"No, indeed," he said. "The hat is covered with dust. It must hang for long periods on the hatrack. And since his wife lets him out the door in such a state, she cannot care much for him."

"Perhaps he is a bachelor, Holmes," I said.

"Why, of course not, Watson. The *H. B.* of that hat clearly fits with the *'Mrs. Henry Baker'* written on the goose's tag."

"True, but will any of this information help you find Mr. Baker?"

"One never knows which information will turn out to be useful," replied Holmes in a matter-of-fact tone. "For the moment, I think an ad in the evening papers will bring the quickest results. Would you be so kind as to hand me a pen and a slip of paper?"

With these, Holmes penned the following message:

> *Found, at the corner of Goodge Street and Tottenham Court Road, a goose and a black felt hat. Mr. Henry Baker can have the same by applying at 6:30 this evening at 221B Baker Street.*

He had just finished putting this to ink when the door burst open. Peterson rushed in, flushed and struggling to catch his breath. "Mr. Holmes, the goose," he choked out, "the goose."

"What about the goose, my good man? Has it risen up and flown away?"

"No, sir," Peterson stammered, his eyes round and almost entirely black. "Look at what my wife found in the goose's throat." He held out his hand, and there in his palm lay a glittering blue gem. It was smaller than a bean. But it was so deep and pure in color that it seemed to glow.

Holmes could hardly contain his excitement. "By George, man, do you know what you have?"

"It must be a diamond, Mr. Holmes. It cuts glass as if it were butter."

"It's the Countess of Morcar's blue carbuncle!" I cried, astonished.

"Precisely," said Holmes, taking the stone from Peterson's outstretched hand. "Usually the stones cut in this rounded shape are red rubies, but this gem, rarest of the rare, is blue. The countess has offered a thousand pounds for its reward. And that is not even a twentieth of its price!"

Peterson sat down, almost in a faint. "A thousand pounds?" he gasped.

"If I recall correctly," I remarked, "the carbuncle was stolen from the countess's room less than a week ago."

"Exactly," said Holmes. "I saved the newspaper account so I could follow the progress of the case.

Here it is. The details of the robbery are as follows: The Countess of Morcar has recently been staying at the Hotel Cosmopolitan. On December twenty-second a leak was discovered in the countess's dressing room. Mr. James Ryder, the hotel manager, called in a plumber, Mr. John Horner, to fix the leak. Ryder stayed in the room with the plumber as he worked. Then, as Horner was finishing the job, Ryder was called away briefly. The manager left Horner alone in the room, and when he returned, the man was gone."

Holmes scanned the paper and went on. "Ryder saw that drawers were pulled out, and the countess's jewel box was open on the dressing table. He called out, and Miss Catherine Cusack, the countess's personal maid, came running. She checked the box and found the blue carbuncle was missing.

"The manager then sounded the alarm, and the plumber was arrested only a few blocks away, apparently on his way home. Horner struggled frantically and insisted he was innocent. The police did not find the gem on him or in his rooms. The man, though, has a known history of robbery. So Horner was arrested and is awaiting trial." Holmes folded the newspaper and set it down.

"The question then remains," I said, "how did the gem end up in the goose's throat? The hotel is quite a distance from Tottenham Court Road."

"That's true," Holmes responded, rising from the couch. "It seems that our conclusions about the hat, Watson, may prove more important than we thought."

Peterson was looking dazed. "Peterson," Holmes said, handing the man the advertisement, "we may be able to resolve all this when we hear from Mr. Baker. Kindly run down and put this ad in the late edition of the papers. Then we'll wait to see the results."

"Very well, sir," Peterson said, humbly gazing at the jewel in Holmes's hand. "And the gem?"

"I'll keep the carbuncle here, thank you. And, I say, Peterson," said Holmes, "buy a goose on your way back. We must have one to give our caller when he comes."

Once Peterson had gone, Holmes took the carbuncle to the frosty window and held it up in the sunlight. "It's a fine jewel," he said in a thoughtful tone. "Not surprising that it inspired a crime. Every good gem does. Jewels are the devil's favorite bait."

"'Tis a bonny thing," I agreed.

"This stone was found in China," Holmes explained. "It has only been out of the earth twenty years, and already there have been two murders, a suicide, and several thefts over it. I'm going to put it in the safe and write a note to the countess to tell her we have it."

"Do you think the plumber Horner is innocent?"

"It's too early to say," Holmes replied. "I'll await more data before I draw any conclusions."

"And what of Mr. Henry Baker?"

"I have a hunch," said Holmes, "that Mr. Baker knew nothing of the crime. A man capable of stealing the blue carbuncle would be more careful with his hat and goose. But if Mr. Baker comes tonight, I'll give him a very simple test. Then we'll know for sure."

Having finished his note, Holmes pulled out his violin to play one of Beethoven's sonatas, and I made my exit. I had plenty of time to visit patients before the evening's excitement would begin.

—— ❧ ——

At about six-thirty I returned to Baker Street. I was just taking off my coat when a knock came at the door.

"Mr. Baker, I presume?" Holmes asked, holding the door open to let a tall, older gentleman in.

"It is I," the man said formally. His shoulders were rounded and his head, large.

"I believe this is your hat," Holmes said, handing him the black bowler.

"Yes, sir," he said gratefully, "that is undeniably mine."

"I'm glad to return it," said Holmes. "But as for the goose, I was forced to eat it."

"What! You've eaten it!" Baker cried in dismay.

"Yes," Holmes confirmed. "Or it would have spoiled. But there is a goose on the sideboard that you will find equally delicious, I hope. It's yours if you wish."

"Oh, thank you, sir," Baker sighed in relief. "That will do very well. I'd have hated to go home empty-handed. It would have been hard on my wife. Extra coins have not been as plentiful in our house as they once were."

"I understand," said Holmes. "However, we did save the feathers, legs, and gullet of the other bird. If you want them . . ."

Baker burst into a hearty laugh. "Why, no, sir, that

fine bird will be quite enough. I thank you kindly." He took the goose and started for the door.

"Would you mind telling me where you purchased the goose we ate?" Holmes asked casually. "I've never tasted a finer bird."

"Not at all," replied Baker. "Some friends of mine often meet at the Alpha Inn tavern. Over the last year, we all deposited a few pence each week with the innkeeper, Mr. Windigate. Then, on the day before Christmas, Mr. Windigate took the money and bought each of us a fancy gander. And the rest you well know." With a solemn bow, he bid us good day.

After Baker had left, Holmes pulled out his coat and hat. "Watson, are you hungry? I suggest we follow up this clue while it's still hot and head to the Alpha Inn for supper."

"By all means," I replied, curious to see where our investigation would take us.

The snow crunched under our feet as we made our way to the Alpha Inn.

"What'll you have?" the landlord barked as we entered the dark tavern.

"Two beers," Holmes answered, "if your beers are as good as your geese."

The man's ruddy face wrinkled in surprise. "You've heard of the Goose Club? Well, sir, them's not *our* geese. I picked them up from a chum at Covent Garden. Mr. Breckinridge has always done me right."

Holmes smiled. "Well, then, to his health and yours!"

After downing our beers along with a fine pub meal, we tipped our host and headed for the Covent Garden Market. We arrived just as Breckinridge was closing his stall for the evening.

When Holmes inquired about the Alpha Inn geese, the grocer burst out in anger, "I'm all out of geese, can't you see? I'm sick of all these questions about geese: 'Where are the geese?' 'Who'd you sell the geese to?' 'What's the price of them geese?' I'm closing, and I won't answer any more questions about geese." His plain, horsey face was pinched from the cold, and he turned his back on us.

But Holmes persisted, "I don't know who's been asking you questions, but I've got a fiver on your answer. I know the goose I ate was country bred, and I've got to find a way to prove it."

The man twisted around abruptly and snapped, "You needn't waste your time, mister, because you're wrong. Those geese were town bred or my name ain't Breckinridge."

"I know a country fowl when I eat it," argued Holmes, "and that's what it was. You can't make me the fool."

The man laughed harshly in his face. "You're making yourself the fool. If you want to lose some money on top of it, you can make a bet with me. A sovereign says they were town bred."

"A sovereign it is," Holmes retorted, pulling a golden coin from his pocket.

"Ha!" Breckinridge shouted triumphantly, pointing

to the cramped scribbling in his books. "Look down this column, and what do you see? *Mrs. Oakshott/ 117 Brixton Road. December 22—24 geese. All sold to Mr. Windigate/Alpha Inn.*"

Holmes slammed the coin angrily down on the counter and left without another word. A few steps away Holmes began to chuckle softly. "A wager works every time. Mr. Breckinridge gave us all the information we —"

Holmes's remark was cut short by a loud hubbub from the stall we had just left. We turned to see Breckinridge swinging his broom at a small, thin man.

"There was only one black-tailed gander, and it was mine," the man screamed, as he ducked from the grocer's swinging blows. "Mrs. Oakshott gave it to me, and I mean to get it."

"All you'll get is the end of my stick," Breckinridge yelled back. "If you don't quit bothering me, I'll set my dog on you and whistle for the police."

Frightened, the man scuttled off into the darkness.

"Sounds like that man wants the very goose we cooked," Holmes said, his brows drawn together in thought. "We'd better come to the end of our trail before the thief knows we're on it."

"But, Holmes," I said, pulling my coat closer around my neck, "who's the thief? Do you think that man is a friend of the plumber? And how do you suppose the jewel ever got into the neck of the goose? I must admit that I am puzzled."

"Patience, my dear Watson," said Holmes. "We're on our way to finding the precise answers for all those questions."

We hailed a cab to Brixton Road and came to Mrs. Oakshott's farm. We knocked at the door of the small stone house, and a young woman answered.

"What is it you want?" she asked.

"Excuse me, ma'am," said Holmes politely. "I was just down at Covent Garden looking for a goose, and a man there sent me to ask you if you had any left. My mother has just come from the hospital and would dearly love a taste of Christmas goose."

She looked at us cautiously. "Who was this man who sent you to me?"

"I didn't quite catch his name," said Holmes, looking innocent. Then he went on to describe the man we had seen arguing with Breckinridge. "He said that he had got a luscious black-tailed gander from you, and that I couldn't do better."

"Ah, that's my brother Jimmy you met," Mrs. Oakshott said, her face relaxing into a smile. "Jim Ryder. I'm surprised he sent you to me. I fatten up a good goose for him, but he doesn't want it. Instead he comes down here a day before Christmas and looks at the geese while I'm in the house. Then he tells me his heart is set on a different goose—the gander with the black tail. So I catch it for him, and a day later, back he comes, telling me I gave him the wrong gander. He's all upset and asks me why I didn't tell him there was another black-tailed gander in the bunch. Why should he care? Then when I tell him that I sold the rest of that batch of birds to Mr. Breckinridge, he runs out of here angry as a hornet. Yes siree, he's been acting mighty strange lately, that brother of mine."

Holmes's face lit up as she talked. "Well, Mrs. Oakshott, I'd be glad to take any one of the birds from another batch, and I'll pay you well for it."

She happily agreed to this, and we were soon on our way with a goose in hand.

"Watson," Holmes said with glee, "the case has now come full circle. We've been led straight back to the Hotel Cosmopolitan."

At ten o'clock the next morning, Sherlock Holmes and I took a cab to the Hotel Cosmopolitan. We had an appointment to talk with the manager, James Ryder.

When we arrived, we were led into a small study to wait for him. A slender gentleman with sloped shoulders and a thin, snoutlike nose soon entered. I saw immediately that he was the man who had been at Breckinridge's stall.

"And what may I do for you, gentlemen?" Ryder asked us, walking around behind his desk. He clasped his hands together nervously.

Holmes smiled politely. "We realize, Mr. Ryder, that you are a very busy man, so we will only take up a few minutes of your time. We heard that you were looking for a particular black-tailed goose."

Ryder swallowed, and his face turned pale. "Why, yes," he said slowly. "How did you hear of it?"

"We happened to overhear you at Mr. Breckinridge's stall. It just may be that we have eaten your bird." Holmes's eyes were glimmering with humor. "And a most remarkable bird it was. It laid one of the bonniest blue eggs I ever laid eyes on." Out of his pocket, Holmes drew the shining blue carbuncle.

Ryder did not move. He did not breathe. I kept my hand in my pocket, lightly touching the pistol Holmes had asked me to bring. Finally, Holmes said, "The game's up, Mr. Ryder."

Ryder ran from behind the desk, and I pulled the pistol from my pocket as he went for Holmes. But, suddenly, to our surprise, Ryder dropped to his knees.

"Grant me mercy, Mr. Holmes," he begged. "I've never stolen anything before. Think of my mother and my sister! And my father would die of shame.

Please, kind sir, do not bring me to court!"

"Get up, man," said Holmes, pulling him to his feet.

Ryder hung his head and collapsed in the closest chair. "It was Catherine Cusack, the maid, who started it all," he cried. "She came to me and asked me to do it. God help me!" He began to sob softly.

Holmes put a hand on his shoulder. "We know many of the details, Mr. Ryder, but it would help for you to tell us what happened."

Ryder looked up, eager to please. "Catherine told me that I only needed to find a workman with a history of robbery. If I did that, she would arrange for something to go wrong in the countess's room. We could then hire the workman, steal the jewel, and blame the theft on him. So I did what Catherine asked. Everything worked fine until she gave me the gem for safekeeping. I was so nervous, I panicked."

Ryder's voice filled with despair. "I was too afraid to carry the gem or hide it at my house. So I went straight to my sister's, thinking I could hide it there somewhere. Josephine had promised me a Christmas goose, and as I was staring at her geese, an idea came to me. Geese can eat anything! So I chose a gander with an unusual black pintail and shoved the gem down its throat. But then the goose got away. So I asked Josephine to give me the black-tailed gander for Christmas. And she did, but she didn't tell me she had two ganders with the same markings. She gave me the wrong one and then sold the rest of the flock. When I discovered the mistake, I went to talk to the grocer.

I thought I could recover the goose, but he wouldn't tell me where it had gone."

"As I had suspected," said Holmes.

"Please let me go free, Mr. Holmes," Ryder begged. "I've never done anything wrong before. Nor will I again. And I'll leave the country. The plumber will go free if I'm not here to testify against him."

Holmes was silent as the man whimpered in his chair. Then Holmes said to him, "Get out, sir, and let this be the last I see of you."

Tears filled the man's eyes once more. "Ah, thank you, sir. Heaven bless you." Then Ryder pulled out his handkerchief, wiped his face, and walked from the room. James Ryder was never heard from again.

Holmes looked at me and shrugged. "Well, my dear Watson, Ryder's no criminal. If I send him to jail, I make a jailbird of him for life. And 'tis the Christmas season, after all."

Smiling thoughtfully, Holmes put the gem back in his pocket, and we went upstairs to talk to the countess in private. Horner was later set free, and the case was closed for lack of evidence.

The goose chase is now over, and Holmes has once again solved the case. Could you have found the culprit on your own? Check the **CLUES,** *and see if you followed every turn in Holmes's reasoning. You may find you've made some important deductions of your own.*

CLUES
that led to the solution of *The Blue Carbuncle*

While reading the newspaper account of the theft, Holmes noted that both the plumber, John Horner, and the manager, James Ryder, had spent a brief time alone in the countess's dressing room. Therefore, either man could have stolen the jewel. So Holmes had at least two suspects.

Since Henry Baker dropped the goose, Holmes figured that he had not been aware of the treasure he was carrying. This theory was confirmed when Baker accepted a new goose in exchange for the old one and laughed at the idea of taking the original goose's remaining parts. Baker could have acted this way because he suspected Holmes's trap. But Holmes thought this was a slim possibility considering the man's careless nature.

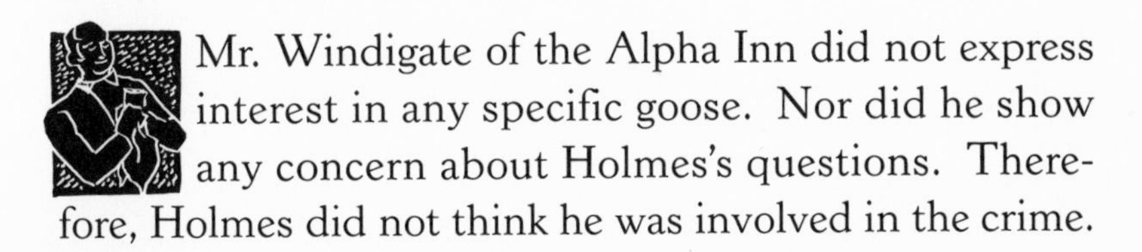

Mr. Windigate of the Alpha Inn did not express interest in any specific goose. Nor did he show any concern about Holmes's questions. Therefore, Holmes did not think he was involved in the crime.

Breckinridge refused to tell Holmes where his geese had come from. So Holmes thought the grocer could have something to hide. He therefore tested Breckinridge by using a wager to draw out information. If the man were guilty, a small bet would not have been enough to make him reveal the information Holmes needed.

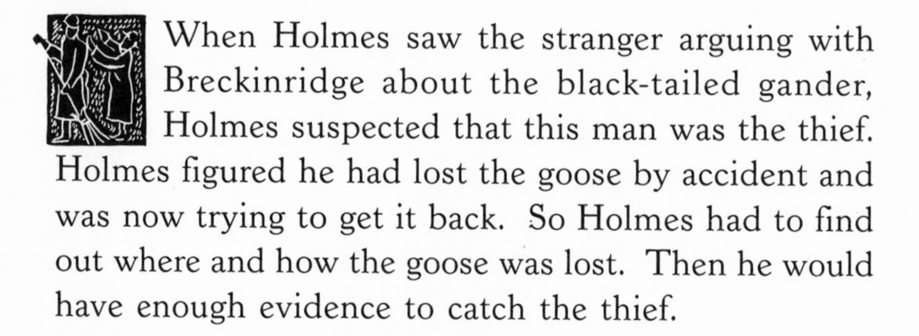

When Holmes saw the stranger arguing with Breckinridge about the black-tailed gander, Holmes suspected that this man was the thief. Holmes figured he had lost the goose by accident and was now trying to get it back. So Holmes had to find out where and how the goose was lost. Then he would have enough evidence to catch the thief.

When Mrs. Oakshott told the story of the look-alike black-tailed ganders, Holmes knew she was innocent. He suspected that her brother had placed the gem in the throat of one of the ganders, and that she had given him the wrong one without knowing it. This was confirmed by Ryder's confession.

The Arms of the Honorable City of London
Skye
Inverness
Aberdeen
Dundee
Glasgow
221
BAKER
Regent's park
Road
Hampstead Road
City Road
Euston Rd.
Edgware
Clerkenwell Rd.
British Museum
221
Baker St.
b
Law Courts
Guildhall
Marylebone Road
Road
Bishopsgate
Aldgate
Marble Arch
Picadilly Circus
St. Paul's Cathedral
Bond St.
Hyde park
THAMES RIVER
Picadilly
Knightsbridge
a
Green park
St. James
LONDON
Irish Sea
York
North Sea
Leeds
Hull
Liverpool
Manchester
a
The Adventure of The Six Napoleons
KENNINGTON RD., LONDON
Stoke-on-Trent
Wolverhampton
St. George's Channel
Norwich
Birmingham
Northampton
Hereford
Ipswich
b
The Blue Carbuncle
TOTTENHAM CT. RD., LONDON
Oxford
Cardiff
London
Bath
Taunton
Salisbury
Tunbridge Wells
Exeter
Dartmoor
Brighton
Portsmouth
Bournemouth
Plymouth
The ENGLAND of Sherlock Holmes